Copyright © 1989 by Nord-Süd Verlag, Mönchaltorf, Switzerland.
First published in Switzerland under the title *Olli, der kleine Elefant*. English
translation copyright © 1989 by Rada Matija AG. North-South Books English language
edition copyright © 1989 by Rada Matija AG, 8625 Gossau ZH, Switzerland.

10   9   8   7   6   5   4   3   2   1

First published in the United States, Great Britain, Canada, Australia
and New Zealand in 1989 by North-South Books, an imprint of Rada Matija AG.

Library of Congress Catalog Card Number: 89-42608.

British Library Cataloguing in Publication Data

Bos, Burny, *1944*–
    Olli, the little elephant.
    I. Title   II. Beer, Hans de, *1957*–   III. Olli, der
    kleine Elefant.   *English*
    833'.914[J]
    ISBN 1-55858-012-3

Ollie
the Elephant

Written by Burny Bos
Illustrated by Hans de Beer

North-South Books
New York

When Ollie the elephant celebrated his birthday there was a big party. His mother baked a wonderful cake, with peanut butter icing. His friends brought him many, many presents, including a drum, a trumpet, a doll, a ball and even two pairs of roller skates. But Ollie was not happy.

After all the guests had left, his mother gently asked him what was wrong.

"I like my presents," said Ollie, "but what I really wanted for my birthday was a baby brother."

Ollie's mother looked down at him and shook her trunk. "You don't get little children for your birthday. You have a new doll, why don't you pretend that he's your baby brother?"

Ollie still wasn't happy, so he strapped on his skates and rolled away to find a baby brother.

After Ollie had skated for a while he met a stork. "Good morning, Mrs. Stork," said Ollie. "Can you give me one of your little ones? I want to have a baby brother to play with."

"Of course not," said the stork. "I love all my children very much. I won't give any of them away."

Ollie was quiet for a moment. Then he looked up at the stork's empty nest and had an idea. "May I sit in your nest for a while? Maybe I'll see a baby brother."

The stork looked at Ollie kindly. "I'll be happy to get some friends and fly you up to my nest, but you won't get a baby brother that way."

"We'll see about that," said Ollie.

The storks put Ollie into a blanket and flew him up to the nest. He sat for an entire hour, but he was too scared to look down so he didn't find a baby brother.

Happy to be back on solid ground again, Ollie continued on his journey. It was almost dark when he came to a junk heap in the forest where he met a stag.

"Hello, Mr. Stag," said Ollie. "Do you have children?"

The stag looked puzzled. "Yes, I have several beautiful children."

"Great!" said Ollie. "I want a baby brother. May I join your family?"

"I'm very sorry," said the stag, "but you wouldn't really fit in. You should go home to your own mother and father. It's getting late and they must be worried about you." With that, the stag bounded off into the forest.

Ollie sat down on an old sofa and thought for a moment. Then he had an idea. He broke an old chair and tied it on his head. "Perfect," said Ollie. "Now I'll fit right into Mr. Stag's family."

Ollie skated through the forest, but he couldn't find his new family. It became dark and Ollie was very tired, so he took off his skates, curled up under a tree, and went to sleep.

When Ollie woke up it was a bright, beautiful new day. He took the chair off his head, put on his roller skates and went on his way. Suddenly, a frog leaped across his path.

"Hey there," called Ollie. "I'm trying to find a new family. May I come and live with you?"

The frog thought for a moment. "Well, I already have hundreds of children, so I guess another one won't be too much trouble. Take off your skates and I'll show you where we live."

Ollie was very happy. The frog hopped onto Ollie's head and Ollie trotted off to the pond.

Ollie jumped into the water and sat on the bottom with his trunk sticking out so that he could breathe. But as he looked around at the frog and all the other pond creatures, he began to wonder if this was the right home for him.

Reluctantly, Ollie stood up and climbed out of the pond. "I'm sorry Mrs. Frog," he said sadly. "Your pond is perfect for frogs, but it's not the right place for me."

Ollie put on his roller skates and rolled away, dripping wet and very unhappy.

As it began to get dark, Ollie came to a town. He crept inside a small building and there he met a large striped cat.

"What's wrong?" asked the cat. "You look very sad."

"I'm lost!" said Ollie. "I ran away from home to find a baby brother and now all I want is to go home to my mother."

"I remember being lost when I was little," said the cat as she licked her paws. "Follow me and I'll show you what to do to find your mother."

Ollie skated along behind the cat until they came to a wall. "Here we are," said the cat. "Climb up on this wall and meow until your mother comes to get you."

Ollie thanked the cat for her help and she trotted off to feed her kittens. He looked up into the sky and called for his mother over and over, but she didn't come.

He was very tired, so he climbed down and hid behind some bushes. As he started to go to sleep he decided that maybe his mother was angry and didn't want him anymore.

The next morning Ollie was walking across a field when suddenly the ground below him caved in.

"Hey buster!" shouted a badger. "You've ruined our baby's den! It took us hours to tunnel out that room!"

"The baby is due any day now," sighed the mother badger. "What are we going to do?"

Ollie apologized to the badgers. "I'll be happy to dig out a new den. I love babies and I certainly don't want yours to have to sleep outside."

So Ollie dug and dug and dug and soon the badgers had a new den that was even better than the first.

"You're a good little elephant," said the father badger. "I'm sure your mother is very proud of you."

When he heard this, Ollie almost started to cry. He said goodbye to the badgers and slowly walked away.

As he walked along, Ollie met a beautiful peacock. The peacock asked him why he looked so sad and Ollie told him his story. "I'm sorry I can't help you find a baby brother," said the peacock, "but I can think of a way to cheer you up."

The peacock gathered a few feathers from all of his friends and tied them around Ollie's waist. "There you go," said the peacock. "Now you're the most beautiful elephant in the whole world."

Ollie was very happy. He held up his head proudly and continued on his journey.

Ollie's happiness did not last long. One by one the beautiful feathers fell out, and soon he was just a lonely little elephant again. By evening he was completely lost, and he also realized that he had left his roller skates in the town.

Suddenly, he heard a strange screeching sound and when he turned around he saw a bat. "You look very sad," said the bat. "Is there anything I can do to help?"

The little bat listened very patiently as Ollie explained his problem. "Well," said the bat, "I can't help you find a baby brother, but the least I can do is offer you a place to rest. Why don't you come and hang out with my family?" Ollie happily accepted the offer, but he didn't realize quite what the bat had meant.

Although it was very hard, Ollie was finally able to hang upside down with the bats. As Ollie tried to rest, the kind little bat flew around and offered some advice. "Your mother must be very worried about you. I'm sure she loves you very much. I can tell you how to get back to the town where you left your roller skates. You should go and get them and skate right back home where you belong."

On his way back to town Ollie met a kangaroo, who had a baby in her pouch. When Ollie told her his story she offered to let him play with her baby. She tied a blanket around Ollie's belly and the baby kangaroo jumped right in.

Ollie was so happy that he forgot about being homesick. He sat down with the baby kangaroo and told him how much he wanted a brother of his own.

Soon it was time for the kangaroos to leave. The baby jumped back in his mother's pouch. They said goodbye to Ollie and bounded off.

After he found his roller skates, Ollie tried to remember how to get back home, but soon he was lost again. Ollie came upon a woodpecker making a nest and asked him for help.

"I can give you directions," said the woodpecker. "I've flown by your house many times. But it's almost dark, so why don't I make us both a nest and tomorrow I'll tell you how to get back home."

The next morning Ollie was very excited. The woodpecker gave him directions and Ollie skated off as fast as he could.

As he came around a curve he was thinking about his mother and how much he missed her when — CRASH! — he ran right into a tree.

When Ollie woke up he saw the kindly face of an elephant looking down at him.

"Mother!" shouted Ollie.

"I'm not your mother, Ollie, I'm Doctor Jumbo. Your mother will be here any minute now."

"Where am I?" asked Ollie.

"You're in the hospital," said the doctor. "You hurt your head and broke your leg when you ran into the tree. I'm afraid you'll have to stay here for a while."

Ollie sighed happily and closed his eyes. Just as he was about to fall asleep his mother came in and gently caressed him with her trunk. "My dear little Ollie," she said softly. "We've been so worried about you."

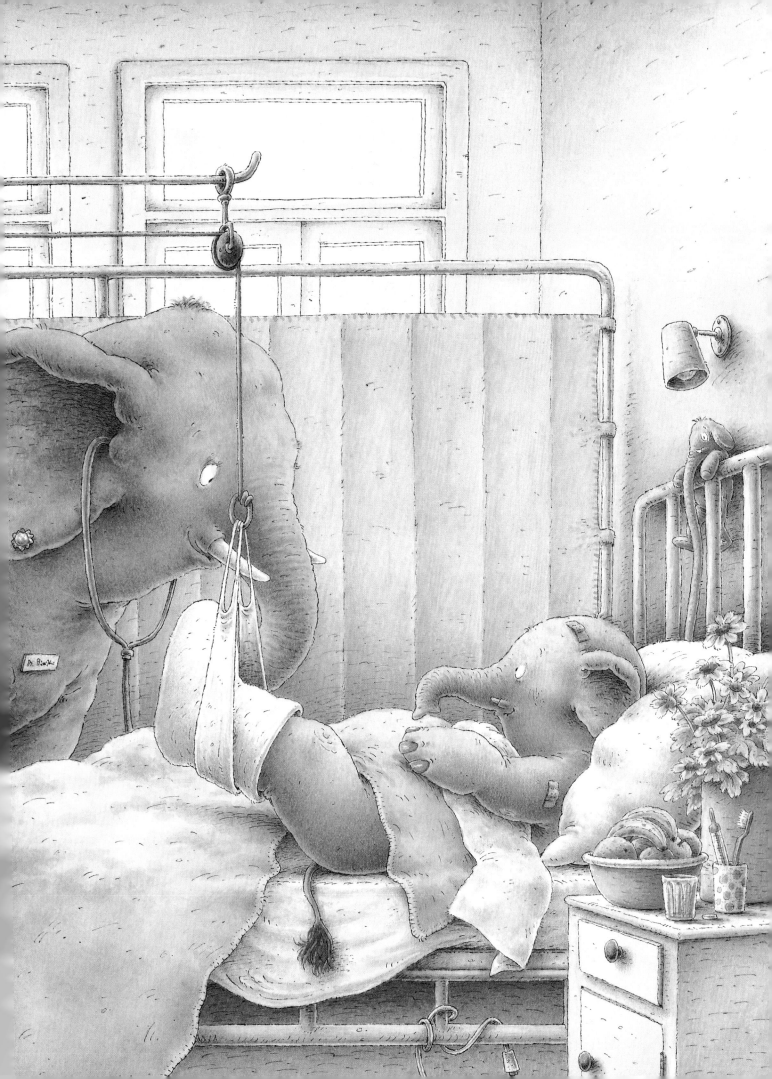

Soon, Ollie was well enough to go for a walk in the park. He told his mother and Doctor Jumbo all about his adventures, especially about the baby kangaroo. This made him very sad, because he still wished he had a baby brother.

"I have some wonderful news for you Ollie," said his mother, smiling. "Your father and I plan to have more children, so someday soon you'll have a baby brother or sister to play with. Would you like that?"

"Yes!" shouted Ollie. "I like baby elephants best of all!"

Ollie hugged his mother and limped back to his room holding her trunk. She tucked him into bed and kissed him on the cheek and when he fell asleep he dreamed of having lots of brothers and sisters to play with.